KINDERGARTEN KIDS

W9-BVL-132

Hooray for the Holidays!

by Catherine Hapka
illustrated by Mike Byrne

Scholastic Inc.

ISBN: 978-0-545-89209-4

10 9 8 7 6 5 4 3 2 1   15 16 17 18 19

Printed in the U.S.A.   40
First printing, 2015
Book design by Carla Alpert

Gavin is in kindergarten.

It is the day before winter break. "Are you all excited for the holidays?" asks Ms. Green.

"YES!" the kids cheer.

"Families celebrate different traditions during the holidays. They pass them on year after year," says Ms. Green.

Abby

"What does your family do for the holidays?" Ms. Green asks. "Draw your family tradition."

Gavin

The kids get to work.
Gavin grabs a green crayon.
He draws a Christmas tree.

Gavin

He draws a present.
A new soccer ball is inside!

Abby looks at Gavin's picture.
"That looks like fun," she says.

Abby

"Thanks," Gavin says.
"I love the holidays."

Gavin

Ms. Green claps her hands.
"It is time to share our traditions."

"Who wants to go first?" she asks.
"Me! Me!" Gavin says.

Gavin shows his pictures.
"My family celebrates Christmas.
We sing carols," he says.
"We put out cookies for Santa."

"This is Christmas morning,"
Gavin says.
"We go to church.
Then we open gifts."

"Good work, Gavin,"
Ms. Green says.
"Who wants to go next?"

Gavin wonders what his friends drew.
Will all the pictures look the same?

Roberto

"My family is Jewish," Ben says.
"We celebrate Hanukkah.
It lasts eight days."

"We light a candle on the menorah every night.
We play a game called dreidel.
We get a present every night, too!"

Jada is next.

"My family celebrates Kwanzaa,"
she says.

"It is an African American holiday.
We celebrate for seven days."

"Kwanzaa honors our history and community.
We light candles on the kinara.
We have red, green, and black balloons."

Next comes Abby.
"My family is from Sweden,"
she says.
"We celebrate St. Lucia's Day."

"It is the shortest day of the year.
So we celebrate light.
Kids wear white and carry candles.
Then we have a parade."

Now it is Roberto's turn.
"My family is from Mexico.
We celebrate Christmas for nine
days."

"We have a piñata," he says.
"It is filled with treats.
We break the piñata and eat the
treats together."

"My family is from Haiti," Jack says.
"We celebrate on Christmas Eve."

"We leave our shoes on the porch.
Santa fills them with presents!"

"It would be fun to share all these traditions," Gavin says. "We will, Gavin," Ms. Green says. "It is time for our holiday party."

"Hooray!" Gavin cheers.
The other kids join in.

Ms. Green leads the way to the lunchroom.
There is a Christmas tree and a menorah.

There is a kinara with candles.
There is a piñata filled with
yummy snacks.
And there are shoes filled with
presents.

"Hooray!" Gavin cries.
"Happy holidays, everyone!"